Way Up The Ucletaw

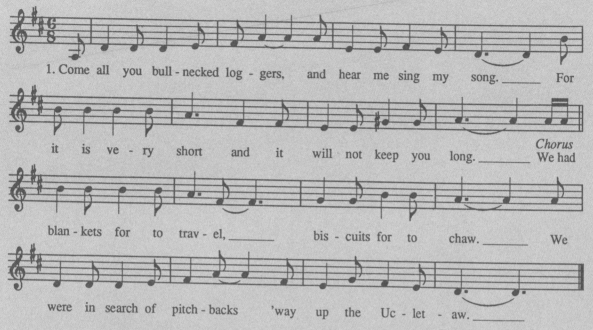

1. Come all you bull - necked log - gers, and hear me sing my song._____ For
it is ve - ry short and it will not keep you long._____ *Chorus* We had
blan - kets for to trav - el,_____ bis - cuits for to chaw._____ We
were in search of pitch - backs 'way up the Uc - let - aw._____

2. We're leaving Vancouver
   With sorrow, grief and woe
   Heading up the country
   A hundred miles or so

3. We hired fourteen loggers
   And we hired a man to saw
   We had a greenhorn cook
   And he run the hotcakes raw

Dedication

To Rolf, my fellow worker and rambler in the woods.
— *Heather*

For all those who work with their hands, and in memory
of John Kelly and my grandfather Lazlo.
— *Claire*

SKOOKUM SAM
SPAR TREE MAN

Story by
Heather Kellerhals-Stewart

Pictures by
Claire Kujundzic

POLESTAR
BOOK PUBLISHERS

Skookum Sam was a wild, west coast logger. Every morning in the cook house, he'd tuck away ten eggs, two dozen hotcakes and a pot of coffee. Then he'd tighten his belt, slap on his hardhat, grab his chainsaw and head for the woods.

Sam sure loved those Douglas fir trees. Before cutting one down, he'd stretch his arms round the gnarly trunk and give it a humongous bearhug. Sometimes Sam would climb a big, old fir and lop off the top to make a spar tree. Know what he would do then?

Darned if that wild west coast logger didn't turn a handstand on top.

One morning, his boss—a ripsnorting, bull-of-the-woods—said to him, "Sam, we won't be needing a new spar tree today."

"But I'm all set to go," Sam said, strapping on his climbing spurs.

"You heard me, Sam. We won't be needing any of your spar trees, now or ever."

"What d'you mean?" Sam asked, flinging his climbing rope round the gnarly trunk of his big, old fir.

"Progress, Sammy-boy. I've got a machine coming up the road here that'll do twice the work in half the time."

Sam's eyes narrowed, his jaw tightened. "No machine's taking over from this logger ... ever." He fastened the climbing rope onto his safety belt, then clipped in his axe and saw.

"Listen here, Sam. Set one foot on that tree and you're fired, understand?"

Well, Sam let go such a holler it frizzled the hair in the boss man's ears. "I'll run circles round your machine."

"I'm warning you, Sam ..."

Sam stared up the length of his old, grandaddy tree. For just one second he felt like a no-see-um sitting on a grizzly bear's snout.

"You can't win out against my steel spar tree, Sam."

"Steel spar tree, huh?" Sam sucked in his breath. When he let go, the blast toppled a nearby sapling and snuffed out the boss man's pipe.

Sam plunged his climbing spurs into the gnarly bark and flipped his climbing rope up.

Thunk, thunk went his spurs. Flip, flip went the rope.

"Sam ... you gone haywire? Get back here."

Sam peered down. From twenty-five metres up that bull-of-the-woods looked mighty puny. Sam hooted and hollered. "I'll beat the pants off any steel spar tree."

"It'll be rigged up and ready before you're anywhere, Sam."

Thunk, thunk went Sam's spurs. Flip, flip went the rope. The first branches were tickling his head. He lopped them off and flipped the rope up.

A bunch of his logging pals gathered below.

"Go, Sammy, go."

"Get back to work," the bull-of-the-woods roared. "What d'you think this is, a holiday camp?"

Thunk, thunk went Sam's climbing spurs. Flip, flip went the rope. He was near halfway up and that steel spar tree below was still flatter than a flapjack without the baking powder.

Sam stopped and reached for his chainsaw. Above him was a rotten, old branch with a raven sitting there. The raven croaked at Sam.

"Thanks for the warning," Sam replied, "but a little bad weather won't hold this logger back."

He let rip with his saw. The chips scattered and down, down sailed that widow-maker branch ... until WHUMP. It hit the ground and exploded like a stick of dynamite.

"Atta boy, Sammy," the loggers cheered.

"Thanks, boys. But I can hardly hear you with the wind thumping my eardrums."

All round him the treetops were a-swinging and a-swaying.

Thunk, thunk went Sam's climbing spurs. Flip, flip went the rope.

"Sam," the bull-of-the-woods roared from fifty metres below, "there's a storm brewing. You hightail it down here."

"Don't see no steel spar tree up yet," Sam hollered back.

"We're quitting work, Sam. And so should you. What are you looking for—a stretcher ride?"

"Come down, Sammy-boy," the loggers echoed. "Better come down."

"Huh," Sam thought, "what do they think this is, a holiday camp?"

Thunk, thunk went his climbing spurs. Flip, flip went the rope. When Sam was higher than all of the other trees he stopped.

Lightning was singeing and scorching the hillsides round about.

Then he told his grandaddy tree, "If I don't get you,
I figure the lightning will, one of these days."

Sam let rip with his saw. Before long the
top of that tree somersaulted over his
head and sailed seventy metres
straight to the ground.

"Come down, Sammy-boy.
Better come down."

"You got it wrong, boys.
I'm holding and hugging
my grandaddy tree just
so I won't come down."

After the shaking and rattling and rolling had stopped, Sam climbed on top. He stood there and belted out an old logger's song his daddy used to sing.

"Come all you bull-necked loggers,
And hear me sing my song,
For it is very short
And it will not keep you long."

They could hear him singing clear down to Vancouver. And all the while the storm was worrying round that tree trunk.
"Come down, Sammy-boy."
"Better come down."

Sam looked north and south. He looked east and west. "Right you are, boys. But it's mighty nice country up this ways and I got one more thing to do."

As Sam was turning a handstand, the lightning bolt struck.

KA—BOOM!

Like a shooting star Skookum Sam flew off into the sky and was never seen again ... Or was he?

Some folks say he's that logger-looking constellation hanging in the western sky. Others claim he fell to earth in some far off place and became a famous trapeze artist.

But when a southeaster is blowing up and sky meets earth, loggers swear they can hear him stomping through the woods. Singing and a-cussing he comes, with a raven black as coal sitting on his shoulder.

"We had blankets for to travel,
Biscuits for to chaw.
We were in search of pitchbacks
Way up the Ucletaw."

And that's the honest truth, it is.

WOOD WORDS

Words are in order of appearance

SKOOKUM: 'tough' or 'strong' in the Chinook jargon, which was a blend of Native Indian, French and English words, used along the west coast.

SPAR TREE: a tree with the top and branches cut off, used in pulling logs from the woods to the landing place where the logs were loaded onto trucks. Steel poles have now replaced trees, and other, newer machines such as grapple yarders are being used in some logging shows.

COOK HOUSE: the cooking and eating area in a logging camp.

HOTCAKES: pancakes.

DOUGLAS FIR: the tallest tree in British Columbia and Canada and one that was most valued by loggers.

BULL-OF-THE-WOODS: the boss logger or foreman.

CLIMBING SPURS: metal spikes fastened to boots and legs which helped the 'high climber' or 'high rigger' to climb up the tree.

CLIMBING ROPE: the rope that held the high climber to the tree trunk and enabled him to climb up.

NO-SEE-UM: a biting fly, much smaller than a mosquito.

HAYWIRE: anything broken or no good, a poor logging show.

RIG UP: to put rigging—blocks and steel cables—on a spar tree, so the felled trees can be pulled to the loading place.

FLAPJACK: pancake.

WIDOW-MAKER: a rotten treetop, loose branch or chunk of bark which can fall on a logger working below.

LOOKING FOR A STRETCHER RIDE: doing something crazy or dangerous that can cause an accident. One of the many woods sayings that has found its way into our language.

SOUTHEASTER: the wind on the west coast which brings heavy rain and often warmer weather in winter.

PITCHBACK: another name for the Douglas fir tree.

Published by:
Polestar Press Ltd., P.O. Box 69382, Station K, Vancouver, B.C., V5K 4W6

Distributed in Canada by:
Raincoast Books, 112 East Third Avenue, Vancouver, B.C., V5T 1C8

The publishers would like to thank the Canada Council and the
British Columbia Cultural Services Branch for their financial assistance.

Canadian Cataloguing in Publication Data

Kellerhals-Stewart, Heather, 1937-
Skookum Sam, spar tree man
ISBN 0-919591-16-7
I. Kujundzic, Claire, 1952- II. Title.
PS8571.E5862S5 1992   jC813'.54   C92-091293-1
PZ7.K44Sk 1992

Book and cover design by Claire Kujundzic
Music typeset by John McLachlan
Printed in Canada by Friesen Printers

*Thanks to Margo Cormack of Page 11 Books in Campbell River for her wonderful support of local writers, to Ken Bostock for reading the story and making suggestions while it was still in a formative stage, to friend Colin Baxter of Canfor for going over it once again, and to Bob Brough of the Eve River Division, MacMillan Bloedel, for taking the time to read the finished story and to pass it on to several modern day "high climbers" for their critical comment. And special thanks to Phil Thomas of Vancouver for his valuable comments and for permission to use the words and music of the old loggers' song "Way Up The Ucletaw" from the P.J. Thomas collection. The song also appears in the book **Songs of the Pacific Northwest** by Phillip J. Thomas, Hancock House, 1979.*

— Heather